The
Preposterous
Rhinoceros or
Alvin's Beastly Birthday

For Christina, thank you!
And for our three cats,
Grey Meow, Toulouse, and Stinker
—R. B.

Henry Holt and Company, Inc.
Publishers since 1866
115 West 18th Street
New York, New York 10011

Henry Holt is a registered trademark of Henry Holt and Company, Inc.

Published in Canada by Fitzhenry & Whiteside Ltd.,
195 Allstate Parkway, Markham, Ontario L3R 4T8.

Library of Congress Cataloging-in-Publication Data
Bender, Robert.
The preposterous rhinoceros, or, Alvin's beastly birthday / Robert Bender.
Summary: Alvin is convinced that his birthday has been
forgotten especially when his mother tries to interest him in
the strange goings-on outside his window.
[1. Birthdays—Fiction. 2. Animals—Fiction. 3. Humorous
stories.] I. Title. II. Title: Preposterous rhinoceros.
III. Title: Alvin's beastly birthday.
PZ7.B43147Pr 1994   [E]—dc20   93-14200

ISBN 0-8050-2806-4

First Edition—1994

Printed in the United States of America on acid-free paper. ∞
1 3 5 7 9 10 8 6 4 2

This book is for ~~⦿⦿⦿⦿⦿~~

whose birthday is on ~~⦿⦿⦿⦿⦿⦿⦿⦿~~

From ~~⦿⦿⦿⦿⦿⦿⦿⦿⦿⦿⦿~~.

The Preposterous

or Alvin's Beastly Birthday

Rhinoceros

Robert Bender

Henry Holt and Company • New York

Nobody remembered my birthday, thought Alvin.

"Why are you so sad?" asked Mom.
"Oh, it's nothing," replied Alvin.

"Why don't you take a look outside? I think I saw a toad driving down the road!"

"I don't feel like going outside!" said Alvin.

"But there's a rhinoceros looking quite preposterous," said Mom.

"...a crocodile wearing a smile...

...and a goat wearing a polka-dotted coat."

"I don't care what's out there. I'm not going out!" said Alvin.

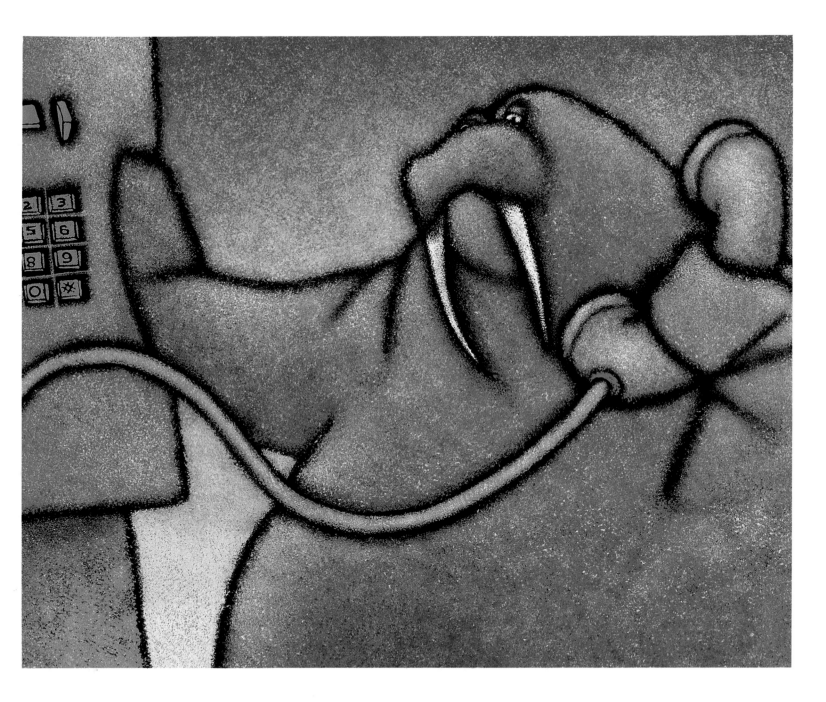

"But there's a walrus trying to call us...

...fish flying out of their dish...

...plus a bug living under a rug...

...an armadillo floating on a pillow...

...and some turtles clearing hurdles."

"What's the point in going outside," protested Alvin,
"when nobody remembered..."

"But there's a pig wearing a wig," said Mom.

...a mouse as big as a house...

...and a snake eating a cake!"

"A cake? What kind of cake?" asked Alvin.
This time he got up and looked out the door to see.

"A birthday cake!" everyone shouted.

Then they all sang happy birthday . . .

HAPPY BIRTHDAY TO YOU!